I Wonder

ANNAKA HARRIS

ILLUSTRATED BY JOHN ROWE

Eva loves to look for the moon. It follows her from place to place, disappearing behind trees and mountains, and then appearing again someplace new.

"Look, Mama, there it is!"

"The moon looks so beautiful in the sky.
How do you think it follows us, Eva?"

Eva thinks about it, but she just can't figure it out.

"It's okay to say, I don't know," says her mother.
"When we don't know something, we get to **wonder** about it!"

"I wonder if the moon and the earth are friends," says Eva.

Her mother smiles. "I like that idea."

"But, Mama, how does the moon *really* stay close to us?"

"There is an invisible force called gravity that pulls all the things in the universe together," Eva's mother explains. "Gravity keeps the moon close to the earth, and it keeps the planets close to the sun, too. They circle around like this."

Eva understands a little better, but then she starts to wonder...

"Mama, where does gravity come from?"

"I don't know, Eva. Nobody really knows for sure. And when no one knows the answer to something, it's called a **mystery**. A mystery is something for everyone to wonder about together."

How fun! Eva imagines herself wondering about gravity together with **all of the people in the world.**

Eva watches the moon disappear behind the clouds
as she walks, excited to see where it will appear next.

"How many grains of sand are in the whole world, Mama?"

"I wonder about that too! There are trillions and trillions
of grains of sand, but nobody knows *exactly* how many."

Eva tries to think about all the sand in the whole world.

"It feels so big that I can't fit it all in my imagination.
It makes me feel dizzy, like I'm falling."

"I know what you mean," her mother agrees,
"and I'm sure other people feel that way too."

Eva walks down another path, looking for the moon,
and a little, orange **butterfly** appears.

Then she notices there are butterflies everywhere!
"Mama, where did all of these butterflies come from?"

"These butterflies have been flying around for a few days. But they started out as little caterpillars. And those caterpillars came from eggs. And those eggs came from *other* butterflies. There are cycles all around us, with one thing ending and another beginning. Things are always changing. Can you think of other things that change?"

"Hmm... Clouds, and frogs...

Later Eva wonders, "Mama, what was here before all the butterflies, and frogs, and clouds – before **everything?**"

"I don't know," answers her mother. "It's another mystery! I like trying to imagine what was here before the beginning of everything. What do you think was here?"

And Eva says, smiling, **"I don't know."**

She thinks about it for a long time, and then she has an idea! "I wonder if there were feelings…"

As she walks home, Eva sees
the moon again, glowing brightly
above the roof of her house.
"Let's go inside and look for
the moon through the window!"

We live with some big mysteries.
When we come upon one, we're given a little gift.
Every mystery is something for all of us to
wonder about together.

What do you wonder about?

Author's Note

I believe that one of the most important gifts we can give our children is the confidence to say "I don't know." It's the foundation from which we begin our investigation of the world: asking questions, taking the necessary time to understand the answers, and searching for new answers when the ones we have in hand don't seem to work. The feeling of not knowing is also the source of wonder and awe.

Before my daughter turned two, she began ignoring questions she couldn't answer. Then she moved on to giving answers she knew to be false. I realized that she had grown accustomed to being celebrated every time she answered a question correctly and was, naturally, less interested in exchanges that didn't produce this response. But I also realized something even more important: I hadn't taught her to say "I don't know" let alone *celebrated* her ability to do so. In all social and emotional learning, children need our help identifying the many new feelings they experience: "Oh, that Batman costume *scared* you," or "I know, you feel *sad* when Mommy leaves." So I went looking for a children's book that would help us talk about the experience of not knowing, but I couldn't find one.

We live in a society where people are uncomfortable with not knowing. Children aren't taught to say "I don't know," and honesty in this form is rarely modeled for them. They too often see adults avoiding questions and fabricating answers, out of either embarrassment or fear, and this comes at a price. When children are embarrassed by or afraid of the feeling of not knowing, they are preoccupied with escaping their discomfort, rather than being motivated to learn. This robs them of the joy of curiosity. Let's celebrate the feelings of awe and wonder in our children, as the foundation for all learning. Let's teach children to say "I don't know" and help them understand the power behind it. Let's talk to them about how it feels to not know something. And, finally, let's be honest with children about the limits of our own knowledge. There is so much for all of us to wonder about together!

~ *For Emma* ~

Thank you to Amy Serkin Lenclos, Dalit Toledano, Amy Rennert, Susan Kaiser Greenland,
Shelley Reicher-Lawrence, Tandy Parks, Jenny Meyer, and most important, my mother, Susan, and my husband, Sam –
this book would not have been possible without your inspiration and guidance.

Published by Four Elephants Press

Book design by Sara Gillingham Studio

Library of Congress Control Number: 2013944719

I Wonder / Annaka Harris; illustrations by John Rowe

Ages one and up

ISBN-13: 978-1-940051-04-8
ISBN-10: 1-940051-04-5